MW01101304

Soccer File
SHOOTING
and
SCORING

by James Nixon

Photography by Bobby Humphrey

A+

Smart Apple Media

Published by Smart Apple Media
P.O. Box 3263, Mankato, Minnesota 56002

U.S. publication copyright © 2012 Smart Apple Media.
International copyright reserved in all countries. No
part of this book may be reproduced in any form
without written permission from the publisher.

Printed in the United States of America at Corporate
Graphics, in North Mankato, Minnesota.

Published by arrangement with the
Watts Publishing Group Ltd., London.

Library of Congress Cataloging-in-Publication Data
Nixon, James, 1982-
  Shooting and scoring / James Nixon; photography by
Bobby Humphrey.
    p. cm.
  Includes index.
  ISBN 978-1-59920-530-4 (library binding)
  1. Hockey--Scoring. I. Humphrey, Bobby. II. Title.
  GV848.3.N59 2012
  796.962'2--dc22

                                        2010042420

Planning and production by
Discovery Books Limited
Editor: James Nixon
Design: Blink Media

The author, packager and publisher
would like to thank the children of
Farsley Celtic Junior Football Club
for their participation in this book.

1020
2-2011
9 8 7 6 5 4 3 2 1

Photo acknowledgements:
Getty Images: pp. 5 top (Laurence Griffiths), 8
(Alex Grimm/Bongarts), 11 (Bongarts), 13 bottom
(Andrew Yates/AFP), 21 top (Nicholas Kahm/AFP),
22 bottom (Daniel Garcia/AFP), 23 bottom (Vladimir
Rys/Bongarts), 28 top-right (AFP); Istockphoto.com:
p. 14 top; Shutterstock: pp. 4 (Jonathan Larsen), 5
bottom (Lario Tus), 15 top (Shawn Pecor), 15 middle
(Jonathan Larsen), 17 left (George Green), 19 top
(Brandon Parry), 21 bottom (Andreas Gradin), 22 top
(George Green), 25 bottom (Sport Graphic), 26 top
(Adam Gasson), 26 left (Jonathan Larsen), 26 right
(Sportsphotographer.eu), 27 left (Alvaro Alexander),
27 right (Sport Graphic), 28 top-left, bottom left
(Jonathan Larsen), 27 bottom-right (Matt Trommer),
29 left (Laszio Szirtesi), 29 right; Wikimedia: p. 20 top.

Cover photos: Shutterstock: left (Sandro Donda),
right (Sportsphotographer.eu).

Every attempt has been made to clear copyright.
Should there be any inadvertent omission please
apply to the publisher for rectification.

Statistics in this book are correct at the time
of going to press, but in the fast-moving world
of soccer are subject to change.

Contents

Words that appear in **bold** are in the glossary on page 30.

SCORING Goals

To win soccer games, you need to score goals. A ball in the back of the net is what the crowd comes to see. A soccer player will tell you there is no greater feeling than the glory of scoring a goal.

The top **strikers** in the game, like Dutch player Ruud van Nistlerooy (below), are experts at scoring goals. This book will show how you can improve your shooting and scoring.

EXPERT: FERNANDO TORRES

Spanish international Fernando Torres is the "complete" striker. This means he has all the skills needed to be a top forward. His speed, **movement**, and skill leave defenders behind and create scoring opportunities. His **finishing** is powerful and accurate. Torres is also excellent at heading, which makes him a danger in the air. Since he joined Liverpool's club in 2007, he has scored an amazing 77 goals in 130 appearances. In 2008, he helped Spain win the European Championship by scoring the winning goal in a 1–0 victory over Germany (right).

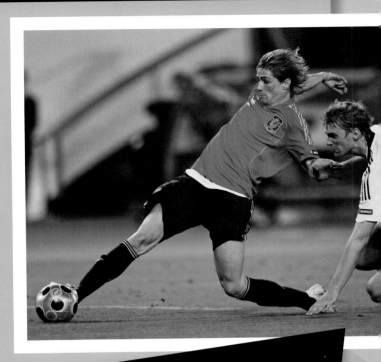

Goal!

Goals can be scored in many different ways. It might be a simple tap-in, a well-placed shot, or a thunderbolt from outside the **penalty box**. It could be a header or a spectacular **volley**. A goal can result from a goalmouth scramble or a lucky deflection. Good strikers have the ability to score all types of goals.

This long-range shot rockets past the goaltender into the top corner of the net.

STRIKING the Ball

To be good at shooting, you need to master the different ways of kicking a soccer ball. You can shoot with the inside, outside, or top (instep) of the foot.

The Basics

▶ Your eyes must be fixed on the ball as you kick it. Look to see where the goal is before you shoot.
▶ Run up at a slight angle, and place your standing foot next to the ball (1).
▶ When you shoot, have your arms spread out for balance (2).
▶ Strike the ball through the middle, and always follow through with your leg (3).

Chip Shot

If the goalie is off his or her line, you can try a chip shot to **lob** them (left). With a sharp stabbing action, dig your foot into the bottom of the ball and then slide your foot underneath it. This will lift the ball into the air.

Sidefoot

Sidefoot: An accurate shot is more important than hitting the ball hard. A shot with the inside of the foot is great for accuracy. Strikers often choose to sidefoot the ball into the net from close range.

Side of instep: You can maneuver the ball around defenders by using the sides of your instep. The easiest way to curve the ball is to strike the ball just off-center with the inside of your instep. To swerve it the other way is more difficult. To do it, kick the ball off-center with the outside of your instep. Your leg should follow through strongly.

Instep: A shot using your instep is less accurate, but is good for driving a shot with power. For this shot, get your head and knee over the ball, and, with your toes pointed toward the ground, kick the ball with the top of your foot.

Instep

Strike PARTNERSHIPS

Goalscoring is usually the result of a team effort. Teams often play with two strikers. They have to work together to make chances and score goals. Over the years, there have been some very famous strike partnerships.

EXPERTS: EDIN DZEKO AND GRAFITE

In 2009, Bosnian Edin Dzeko (left) and Brazilian Grafite formed one of the most successful strike duos in soccer history. Between them, they racked up an incredible 54 goals in 34 games to help Wolfsburg win the German league championship. These two great finishers are the perfect match. Dzeko is tall and good in the air, while Grafite is fast and skillful. With this blend of skills, they cause trouble for defenders and set up dozens of goals for each other.

Understanding

To make a strike partnership work, you have to develop an understanding with your partner. You must be able to predict what they will do next. This will put you one step ahead of the defenders.

The one-two pass (below) is a good way for strikers to work together.

Pass one

Pass two

Combos

The combination of a strong **target player** and a quick forward often works well. The target player is the focus of the offensive play. They win the ball as it is played forward and then knock it down or head it on for a quick forward to run to (right) and score. Some strike partnerships have one forward who hangs back near the midfield. These players need to be creative and set up scoring chances for the strikers ahead of them.

Target player

9

POACHING

Top strikers are good at anticipating where the ball will fall in the penalty box. They have a knack for being in the right place at the right time.

As a result, they score lots of close-range goals. Players with this ability are known as goal poachers.

Poaching Tips

▶ Be ready for rebounds. Always follow your teammates' and your own shots in on the goaltender. They may drop it.

▶ If the defender has to make a **clearance**, run in behind them just in case they miss it.

▶ Poachers need to lose defenders and gain space to shoot. Stay on your marker's shoulder where you can't be seen and lose them with a darting run (left).

Marker

Goalmouth Scrambles

A poacher is good at scoring goals in a crowded penalty box. Their skill is to put the ball in the net in all sorts of ways. They might bundle it in with their chest, deflect it off the side of their head, or **toe-poke** it. It doesn't matter how clumsy it is—a goal is a goal!

EXPERT: BIRGIT PRINZ

German international Birgit Prinz (right) was born to score goals. She is the all-time leading goal scorer in the women's World Cup with 14 goals.

Like all great poachers, she has a good sense of where the goal is. Even with her back to goal, or defenders in her way, she can shoot and find the net.

VOLLEYING

Shooting while the ball is off the ground (volleying) is an important skill for a striker. It saves the player the time it takes to bring the ball under control on the ground.

A volley pulled off correctly can be powerful and spectacular. Volleys are not easy to aim, though. When a ball is spinning quickly toward you in mid-air, it is difficult to make the right contact.

Volley Tips

▶ As the ball comes toward you, get yourself set up in a comfortable and stable position to strike the ball cleanly.
▶ Keep a close eye on the ball, point your toes down, and strike with your instep (1).
▶ Get your body over the ball as you shoot (2). Otherwise, your shot will rise up over the crossbar.

Scissor Kick

If the ball is in the air but you are not facing the goal, you could go for a spectacular scissor-kick shot. Launch yourself into the air with your non-kicking foot, and scissor your legs to strike with the other foot.

Half Volley

The timing of a **half volley** is vital. You need to kick the ball just after it has bounced.

EXPERT: DIDIER DROGBA

Didier Drogba from the Ivory Coast is one of the top strikers in the world. Many of his goals come from volleys. He has great technique when volleying from the side of the goal. He balances on one leg, leans back a little, swivels his hips, and hits the volley with power following through.

HEADING

Heading is a key part of a striker's game. A lot of goalscoring chances come from crosses into the penalty box.

Heading Tips

▸ Do not wait for the ball to reach you. Really attack it.

▸ Time your jump, rise above the ball, and head it at the top of your jump.

▸ Keep the muscles in your upper body tight as you go to head the ball. Doing this will give you power and control.

▸ Pull your neck, head, and shoulders back (1), and meet the ball firmly in the middle of your forehead (2).

▸ Don't shut your eyes when you head the ball.

▸ If possible, head the ball down. It will be harder for the goaltender to save (3).

This forward rises above defenders to head the ball into the net.

1

2

3

PRACTICE DRILL:
Downward Heading

To practice your downward heading, throw the ball against a wall and head the rebound back, aiming for the bottom of the wall.

Glancing Header

If you are not facing the goal, you can glance your header in the right direction. On impact, turn your head toward the target.

Offenders can redirect a cross toward the goal by performing a glancing header.

Diving Header

If a cross is too far in front of you for a normal header or volley, the diving header is an option. Dive forward with speed, lifting both legs off the ground. Be brave, and try to keep your eyes open as you head it.

SET Pieces

Did you know that about a quarter of goals are scored from set pieces? A corner or a free kick just outside the box are dangerous situations for the defense.

The set piece taker has time to whiz the ball across the goalmouth for teammates to attack.

Corner Tips

▸ Aim a corner kick toward an area between the **penalty spot** and the **six-yard box**.
▸ The cross must clear the near-post defender and not be too close to the goaltender or too long either.
▸ Try a near-post corner where a forward moves in front of the defender and flicks it with the top of his head into the middle.
▸ Vary your corners so you don't become too predictable.

1

2

Swing It In

The best technique for corner taking is to bend it with the inside of your instep. Inswinging corners are often hit with speed toward the crowded six-yard box (1). These corners are difficult to clear and only need the slightest touch from a kicker to divert the ball into the net. For outswinging corners, accuracy is more important than speed (2).

Short Corners

An alternative to the cross is the short corner (below). This gives a forward a chance to get a cross in from a closer and better angle.

Goaltender

Goal poacher

Free Kicks

A free kick (see pages 22–23) on the edge of the box is a similar opportunity to a corner. The free-kicker will try to swing the ball into the area between the goaltender and the defensive line for a forward to run on to (below). This is the hardest area to defend.

Attacking Corners

Strikers attacking the corner have to shuffle with their marker and lose them with a well-timed run as the ball comes into the box. A goal poacher usually stands by the goaltender to unnerve them and to try to divert headers into the net (above).

LONG Shots

Long-range shots can result in the most wonderful, eye-catching goals. But more often than not, they end up off target, or they are easily saved. Improving your long-range shooting takes a lot of practice.

Instep Drive

Unless you feel you can curl it into the top corner or lob the goaltender, then the most effective long-range shot is to drive it with your instep (see page 7). This will give you enough power to test the goaltender (right).

To make your shot powerful and low at the same time, get your head and knee over the ball as you shoot (1). Always follow through strongly (2). If you can put curve and spin on the shot, the goalie will have even more trouble saving it.

Long-Shot Tips

- Don't be afraid to shoot. If you see an opportunity, go for it.
- Before you shoot, check the goalie's position. One side of the goal may be left more open than the other.
- Try to catch the goalie off-guard. They may not be expecting a long shot, especially if it is coming through a crowd of defenders.
- The most important thing is to make sure you hit the target and make the goalie do some work.

A long-range shot through a crowd of players can catch the goalie off-guard.

PRACTICE DRILL:
Snap Shot

In a game, you will not have much time to set yourself up for a shot. So you need to practice hitting a moving ball. Get a friend to pass the ball to you on the edge of the penalty area, and try to hit a first-time shot at goal (left).

ONE-on-ONES

A forward will often find themselves near the goal with just the goalie to beat. This is called a one-on-one.

Top strikers score in these situations more often than not. Here are some tips to help you do it:

One-on-One Tips

▸ From close range, it is often good to choose your spot and sidefoot it into the net.

▸ Keep an eye on the goalie. If they move before you kick, you can shoot the other way or even chip it over them (1).

▸ If you are at an angle to the goal, shoot across the goaltender so that any rebound falls into the "danger area" (2).

▸ Try to keep the ball low. It is harder for the goalie to reach down for a low shot.

▸ In training, practice shooting with both feet. This will improve your chances in a one-on-one.

EXPERT: LANDON DONOVAN

Landon Donovan (left) sprints clear of the defense and heads for the goal.

Forwards with speed score lots of one-on-ones. They can outrun the defense when a ball is played over the top or through the back line of defenders. Top U.S. striker Landon Donovan is an expert at this. He hangs onto the shoulder of the last defender and makes his run the moment the pass is played. The timing of the run is crucial to avoid being **offside**.

Rounding the Goalie

The alternative to shooting in a one-on-one is to dribble it around the goalie and tap it into the empty net (right). As the goalie lunges for the ball, you may get tripped, and the goalie will give away a penalty. Do *not* dive and pretend you have been tripped though—you will get a **yellow card**.

FREE-KICK Shooting

A direct free kick just outside the box gives the offensive side a great opportunity to shoot at the goal. The defensive team has to stand at least 10 yards (9.18 m) away from the ball. They will form a wall to block the path to goal. To strike the ball around or over the wall and into the net takes great skill.

Defensive wall

When free-kick takers shoot, they often curl the ball around the wall.

Go for Power

The alternative to a curling shot is to "blast" a free kick. This is a less accurate method, and more likely to hit a defender. But if it does get past the wall, the goaltender has less time to react. A powerful shot could also take a lucky deflection and confuse the goaltender. As the defensive wall often jumps to block a free kick, you can trick them by hitting a hard, low shot.

Curling It

The best way to get the ball around the wall and away from the goaltender is to curl or "bend" it. First, look at where the goalie is standing, and decide where you want to aim. To curl the ball, run up at an angle and hit the ball just off-center with the inside of your instep. If you are trying to get it over the wall, you need to lean back slightly as you strike (right). The spin you put on the ball should help the ball dip back down under the crossbar in time.

Inside instep

EXPERT: CRISTIANO RONALDO

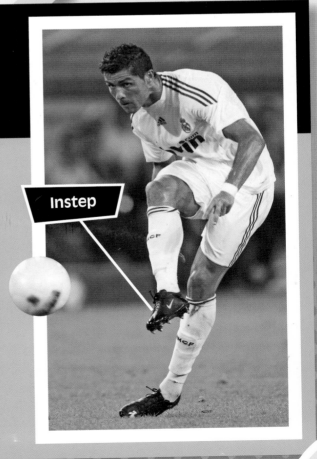

Instep

Cristiano Ronaldo is one of the best free-kickers in the world. He has found a way to shoot with great power and swerve. Watch him and see how he runs straight at the ball and leans right over it as he hits it. He strikes the ball dead center with the upper part of his instep. The bone is quite hard there, so he gets extra power. Hitting the ball hard with this part of the foot also puts topspin on the ball. This puts an amazing dip on the ball, which pulls the shot back down toward the goal once it is over the wall.

PENALTIES

A penalty kick is awarded when a defender commits a foul in their own penalty box. Penalty shoot-outs are used to decide the outcome of a tied cup game.

For the offense, a penalty is the perfect chance to score. The kick is only 12 yards (11 meters) away from goal, and the goaltender cannot move off their line until the ball is kicked.

Keep Practicing

Scoring from a penalty should be straightforward. So how have some of the game's most skillful players missed penalties? The answer is nerves. Under pressure, a player's technique can fail. It is important to practice taking penalties. This will increase your chances of scoring when the time comes and take some of the pressure away. Taking a deep breath before you hit a penalty helps, too.

Penalty Tips

- Decide which way to shoot before you take it. Don't change your mind during your run-up.
- Place the ball on a part of the penalty spot where there are no **divots**.
- You can choose to place the ball firmly with your sidefoot or whack it as hard as possible.

- Shoot into the corners of the goal low or high. Don't shoot at the height of the goaltender—it is easier to save.
- As you take the kick, really concentrate on striking the ball properly and hit it firmly. Don't lean back and "airball" it!

- You could try to trick the goaltender. Before you shoot, look at one corner of the goal, and then shoot the other way (above).

EXPERT: GARETH BARRY

English international Gareth Barry is an awesome penalty kicker. He hits the ball with great power and accuracy into the top corners nearly every time. A penalty into the top corner is impossible to save. But it is the most difficult penalty to pull off.

TACTICS Talk

Wales coach John Toshack instructs his team from the sidelines.

To score goals, a team has to get their forwards or other players into scoring positions. It is no good for a team to have great strikers if the team doesn't make chances for them. Coaches (left) use different **tactics** and **formations** to help their teams take as many shots on goal as possible.

Passing or Direct

If your team does not have possession of the ball, they have no chance of creating a chance and scoring a goal. Some teams play a patient passing game so that they keep possession longer. The players wait until the short passing has opened up space for that final pass to a forward. Some teams try to build attacks and score by playing a more

Teams who use a direct style of play usually have a big target player up front who can win balls in the air. A team with a big forward will also try to get lots of crosses into the box.

direct game. This means they get the ball up to the offense as quickly as they can, playing lots of long balls and fewer short passes in midfield.

Formations

It is important to get used to playing in a variety of formations.

4-4-2: This has been a popular formation for many years. It is used by teams who have a good strike partnership. The two wide midfielders go forward when their team attacks and put crosses into the box.

Englishman Steven Gerrard plays as an offensive midfielder and scores lots of goals.

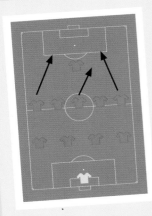

4-5-1: This formation packs the midfield and helps a team keep possession. It has become very popular in recent times. The wide players and one of the central midfielders must make lots of forward runs to support the **lone striker**. Two English midfielders, Frank Lampard and Steven Gerrard (above right), are famous for playing the central offensive midfielder in this system. They score lots of goals by making late runs from midfield into the penalty box. Defenders find it hard to mark these players.

PRACTICE DRILL: 3 on 2

This activity trains you to make the most of scoring opportunities. The offense, with three players, starts with the ball and has to score past two defenders and a goalie. The offense is not allowed to make more than four passes.

STAR Strikers

Here is a rundown of some of the top players in the world today. If your team signs one of these players, expect to see plenty of goals. Each profile contains the player's scoring record for club and country.

Wayne Rooney

D.O.B: 10.24.85
Nation: England
Height: 5'10" (1.78 m)
Weight: 176 lbs (80 kg)
International Caps (Goals) 67 (26)

Club record:		Appearances	(Goals)
2002–2004	Everton	77	(17)
2004–	Manchester United	287	(132)

Sergio Aguero

D.O.B: 6.2.88
Nation: Argentina
Height: 5'7.5" (1.72 m)
Weight: 163 lbs (74 kg)
International Caps (Goals) 25 (8)

Club record:		Appearances	(Goals)
2003–2006	Independiente	53	(23)
2006–	Athletico Madrid	203	(81)

Abby Wambach

D.O.B: 6.2.80
Nation: United States
Height: 5'10" (1.78 m)
Weight: 163 lbs (74 kg)
International Caps (Goals) 147 (117)

Club record:		Appearances	(Goals)
2002–2003	Wash. Freedom (WUSA)	36	(23)
2009–	Wash. Freedom (WPS)	33	(21)

Karim Benzema

D.O.B: 12.19.87
Nation: France
Height: 6 ft. (1.83 m)
Weight: 163 lbs (74 kg)
International Caps (Goals) 31 (10)

Club record:		Appearances	(Goals)
2004–2009	Lyon	150	(68)
2009–	Real Madrid	47	(11)

Fernando Torres

D.O.B: 3.20.84 **Nation:** Spain
Height: 6'1" (1.85 m) **Weight:** 172 lbs (78 kg)
International Caps (Goals) 81 (26)

Club record:		Appearances	(Goals)
2001–2007	Athletico Madrid	243	(91)
2007–	Liverpool	130	(77)

Didier Drogba

D.O.B: 3.11.78 **Nation:** Ivory Coast
Height: 6'2" (1.88 m) **Weight:** 200 lbs (91 kg)
International Caps (Goals) 71 (45)

Club record:		Appearances	(Goals)
1998–2002	Le Mans	72	(15)
2002–2003	Guingamp	50	(24)
2003–2004	Marseille	55	(32)
2004–	Chelsea	273	(138)

Zlatan Ibrahimovic

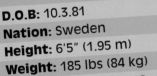

D.O.B: 10.3.81
Nation: Sweden
Height: 6'5" (1.95 m)
Weight: 185 lbs (84 kg)
International Caps (Goals) 66 (25)

Club record:		Appearances	(Goals)
1999–2001	Malmo	40	(16)
2001–2004	Ajax	106	(47)
2004–2006	Juventus	91	(26)
2006–2009	Inter Milan	116	(66)
2009–2010	Barcelona	42	(22)
2010–	Milan	15	(9)

Samuel Eto'o

D.O.B: 3.10.81
Nation: Cameroon
Height: 5'11" (1.80 m)
Weight: 165 lbs (75 kg)
International Caps (Goals) 101 (52)

Club record:		Appearances	(Goals)
1997–2000	Real Madrid	6	(0)
2000–2004	Mallorca	163	(69)
2004–2009	Barcelona	200	(130)
2009–	Inter Milan	62	(33)

Birgit Prinz

D.O.B: 10.25.77 **Nation:** Germany
Height: 5'10.5" (1.79 m) **Weight:** 163 lbs (74 kg)
International Caps (Goals) 205 (126)

Club record:		Appearances	(Goals)
2002	Carolina Courage	15	(12)
2006–	FFC Frankfurt	70	(70)

Landon Donovan

D.O.B: 3.4.82 **Nation:** United States
Height: 5'8" (1.73 m) **Weight:** 148 lbs (67 kg)
International Caps (Goals) 128 (45)

Club record:		Appearances	(Goals)
2001–2004	San Jose Earthquakes	87	(32)
2005–	Los Angeles Galaxy	164	(88)

Statistics in this book are correct at the time of going to press, but in the fast-moving world of soccer are subject to change.

Glossary

clearance a kick or header to move the ball upfield away from the defender's goal

corner a kick taken by the offensive side from the corner of the field after the ball has been sent over the byline by the opposition

cross a long pass from the side of the field into the penalty box

direct free kick a free kick that can be kicked directly into the net without touching another player

divot a small hole in the ground where the grass is missing

finishing the ability to put the ball in the goal

formations the arrangement of a team's players on the field

foul an action that breaks the rules of the game, such as tripping, pushing, handball, etc.

free kick a kick of the ball awarded to a side because of a foul by the opposition

half volley a strike of the ball just after it has bounced off the ground

instep the part of the foot where your shoelaces are

lob to loft the ball over an opponent's head

lone striker a striker who is playing up front on their own with no strike partner

movement a player with good movement makes useful runs and takes up good positions when they are not on the ball

offside a position on the field where the ball cannot be passed to you; to be onside, you must have two opponents between you and the opponents' goal.

penalty box the large rectangular area at each end of the field where the goaltender can handle the ball

penalty shoot-out a contest where each side takes five penalties, sometimes played to decide a tied game

penalty spot the spot marked 12 yards (11 m) from goal where penalty kicks are taken from.

set piece a move done by a team as they return the ball into play, such as a corner or free kick

six-yard box the small rectangular area in front of each goal, where goal kicks are taken

striker an offensive player whose main job is to score goals

tactics the plans and ideas used by a team to gain an edge over the opposition

target player a forward player who receives passes from his or her teammates

toe-poke a kick of the ball with the tip at the front of your shoe

volley a strike of the ball made before it touches the ground

yellow card a warning given to a player by the referee for a bad foul; a player who receives two yellow cards will get a red card and be sent off the field.

Further Information

Books

Soccer Strategies: Attacking, Defending, Goaltending by Paul Fairclough (Firefly Books, 2009)

Teamwork in Soccer by Clive Gifford (PowerKids Press, 2010)

Soccer: The Ultimate Guide by Martin Cloake (DK Pub, 2010)

Striker by Clive Gifford (Sea-to-Sea Publications, 2008)

Web Sites

http://expertfootball.com/training/kicking.php
Get advice on different kicks to use in the game.

http://www.soccer-training-info.com/
Learn how to perfect skills such as volleys and free kicks, plus study soccer strategy.

http://www.soccerxpert.com
This site has shooting tips and drills to help you improve your game.

http://www.abbywambach.com
Read Q&A, watch videos, and get advice from Abby Wambach, named U.S. Soccer Women's Athlete of the Year in 2010.

Index